The Boy Who
Was Followed Home

The Boy Who Was Followed Home

By
MARGARET MAHY
Pictures by
STEVEN KELLOGG

Franklin Watts, Inc. New York 1975

Library of Congress Cataloging in Publication Data

Mahy, Margaret.
    The boy who was followed home.

    SUMMARY: A witch's pill is supposed to cure
Robert of the hippopotami who daily follow him
home from school — but there is one disadvantage to the
treatment.
    [1. Fantasy] I. Kellogg, Steven. II. Title.
PZ7.M2773Bm   [E]   75-4866
ISBN 0-531-02427-X
ISBN 0-531-02834-8 lib. bdg.

5 4 3 2 1

To my nephew Steven
                    S.K.

To Jennifer and
Fiona and Andrew
and Matthew...
four people who are
welcome to follow
me home at any time.
                    M.M.

One day a small, quite ordinary boy, called Robert, was coming home from school. He looked over his shoulder and there was a hippopotamus following him.

Robert was surprised and pleased — pleased because he had always liked hippopotami, and surprised because nothing like this had ever happened to him before.

When he got home the hippopotamus followed him up the steps and tried to come in at the door. Robert thought his mother would not like this, so he shooed it away.

It went and lay down in the goldfish pool on the lawn.

"What on earth is that in the goldfish pool?" asked Robert's father.

"It is a hippopotamus, Father," said Robert.

"Really," said the father. "People should keep their hippos chained up and not allow them to go climbing into other people's goldfish pools."

The next day the hippopotamus followed Robert to school.

Robert was working and playing all day and did not think of the hippopotamus until he went home in the afternoon.

Then there was a rustling noise behind him. When he turned around, there were four hippos following him.

Robert was even more pleased and more surprised than he had been the day before. He was delighted to think that he was the sort of boy hippopotami would follow.

When he got home the hippopotami went and sat in the goldfish pool.

It was quite a big pool, but with four hippos in it, it seemed quite small.

"There are four hippopotami in our goldfish pool this evening," said Robert's mother. "That seems like quite a few."

The next day, the four hippos quietly followed Robert to school, but that afternoon when he walked home nine hippopotami followed him and got into the goldfish pool.

Things went on like this for several days.

Robert's parents, who were very polite, tried to ignore the growing number of hippopotami crowding into the goldfish pool, but when there were twenty-seven hippos jostling each other all over the lawn, Robert's father gave them a gloomy look and said:

"I wonder where they come from?"

"They follow me home from school," Robert said. "They like me."

"There seems to be only one solution for it. We'll have to get a witch to put a spell on you to make you unattractive to hippos."

Robert was sorry because, as you know, he liked hippos, but he had to admit twenty-seven were too many for any lawn.

The father looked up witches in the telephone book and selected Mrs. Cathy Squinge, who advertised children as her specialty.

He made an appointment, and the following midnight, sharp on the broomstick hour, Mrs. Squinge appeared down the chimney.

"Hippo trouble I see," she said, having counted forty-three hippos on the lawn that evening. "A simple pill will solve all difficulties."

"Give it to us quickly," said the father, anxious to get rid of Mrs. Cathy Squinge, who was not very respectable-looking.

"There is one disadvantage perhaps..." began Mrs. Squinge; "the pill does cure people of hippos, but — "

"No buts!" said the father grandly. "Just give us the pill."

So Mrs. Squinge passed the pill to Robert, who swallowed it down.

"The pill is guaranteed," said Mrs. Squinge, "but perhaps I should warn you — "

"Enough!" said the father, and shooed Mrs. Squinge up the chimney.

Sure enough, the next morning the pill worked wonderfully. Although Robert seemed no different, he had no sooner stepped outside than the forty-three hippopotami slunk away from him, giving him reproachful looks over their shoulders.

Within minutes the lawn and even the streets were empty of hippopotami.

Robert couldn't help being a bit sorry, as he was a boy who liked hippos, but off he went to school happily enough.

He played and worked all day, and at last it was time to go home.

As he walked along, he turned around half expecting to see the hippos, but there wasn't a hippo in sight.

Robert was *very* pleased.